UP NEXT)))

:02 **SPORTS ZONE SPECIAL REPORT**

:04 **FEATURE PRESENTATION:**

PAINTBALL PUNK

FOLLOWED BY:

:50 **SPORTS ZONE POSTGAME RECAP**

:51 **SPORTS ZONE POSTGAME EXTRA**

:52 **SI KIDS INFO CENTER**

WOLVES TOP TEAMMATE REFUSES TO PLAY NICE

CHESTER COYOTE

STATS:
POSITION: SCOUT
AGE: 14
TEAM: WOLVES

BIO: Chester Coyote doesn't play well with others. It's not that he's a bad guy — he just doesn't quite get the whole "teamwork" thing. He likes to hang out with his friends, and he loves playing paintball...just not at the same time. If he can't figure out a way to run with the pack against the Riot, this lone wolf will get picked off — and fast.

BLZ vs BKS
3-1
TGR vs RDR
33-32
EAG vs BAN
14-7
SPA vs WLD
4-3
BAN vs RDR
21-15
RZR vs LIG
4-3
BLZ vs BKS
3-1
TGR vs RDR

CORA RAMIREZ

TEAM: WOLVES   AGE: 14
POSITION: POINT

BIO: Cora is the Wolves' team captain and strategist. Her tactical skills are often the difference between victory and defeat for the Wolves. In fact, most of their biggest wins have resulted from her strategies.

PETER ECCLESTON

TEAM: WOLVES   POSITION: MARKSMAN   AGE: 15
BIO: Peter is a professional in the making. He's calm under pressure, an excellent sharpshooter, and he always plays well with others.

ECCLESTON

JACK BOWSER

TEAM: WOLVES   POSITION: ANCHOR   AGE: 14
BIO: Jack's much stronger than the average 14-year-old. As the team's anchor, he lays down cover fire and guards the rear.

BOWSER

THE RIOT

AGES: 13-15
BIO: The Riot are trained by S.W.A.T., an elite police unit. The team hasn't lost a single paintball match in two years.

the RIOT

SEMI-FINALS UPDATE: THE WOLVES AND THE DESTROYERS ARE

PRESENTS

A PRODUCTION OF

STONE ARCH BOOKS
a capstone imprint

written by *Sean Tulien*
illustrated by *Aburtov*
inked by *Andres Esparza*
colored by *Fares Maese*

designed and directed by Bob Lentz
creative direction by Heather Kindseth
editorial direction by Michael Dahl

Sports Illustrated KIDS *Paintball Punk* is published by Stone Arch Books,
151 Good Counsel Drive, P.O. Box 669, Mankato, Minnesota 56002.
www.capstonepub.com

Summary: Chester Coyote is a talented paintball player. Unfortunately, he
would rather be a lone wolf than run with the pack. His team, the Wolves,
is in the state paintball finals, but he isn't seeing eye-to-eye with his best
friend, Cora Ramirez, the team's captain. Chester won't follow her orders,
and his class-clown personality is turning the rest of the pack against
him. If Chester doesn't decide to play well with others, he'll lose his
friends — as well as the paintball championship.

Cataloging-in-Publication Data is available at the Library of Congress
website.

ISBN: 978-1-4342-2219-0 (library binding)
ISBN: 978-1-4342-2788-1 (paperback)

Printed in the United States of America in Stevens Point, Wisconsin.
032010   005741WZF10

MATCH EACH — THIRD AND FINAL MATCH IS IN PROGRESS . . / **SIK** *TICKER*

My name's Chester Coyote.

You can't see me right now.

Where's he hiding?

I'm not sure.

I'm supposed to be backing up my teammates, the Wolves...

Move out!

He came through here.

...but I prefer to work alone.

I avoided my teammates all week.

The next time I saw them, we were facing the Riot in the state paintball championship.

Okay, Wolves. Here's the plan of attack . . .

First, we'll . . .

Jack will cover . . .

Then eter . . .

?

Blee blah bo-dee-dah. a-dee-dah. Blah.

Blee blah bloo-dee-dah.

. . . it's three against Chester!

GULP!

Looks like I'm on my own again.

But that's just how I like it.

A few moments later...

Wolves, are you ready for the second match?

We're ready.

Riot, are you ready?

Affirmative.

TWEEEEET!

TWEEEET!

Let the final match begin!

Each person is different in their own way.

But, like it or not . . .

Do your thing, Chester!

You got it!

. . . we're all part of the same pack.

COYOTE

WOLVES TEAM UP TO SUBDUE RIOT!

STORY: After a rocky start, the Wolves regrouped to take down the Riot in the state paintball finals. After accidentally marking his own teammate in the first match, Chester Coyote made up for his mistake by sacrificing himself to save her in the second match. Cora and the other Wolves rallied behind Chester's selfless act to quickly take out the remaining Riot players. It was smooth sailing from there, as the Riot were eliminated two games to one.

BY THE NUMBERS

MARKS:
OYOTE: 5
AMIREZ: 6

Sports Illustrated KIDS

UP NEXT: SI KIDS INFO CENTER

SZ *POSTGAME EXTRA*

WHERE *YOU* ANALYZE THE GAME!

Paintball fans got a real treat today when the Wolves one-upped the Riot in the state paintball championship! Let's go ask some fans for their thoughts on the day's exciting matchup ...

DISCUSSION QUESTION 1

Which member of the Wolves is your favorite — Cora, Chester, Jack, or Peter? Why?

DISCUSSION QUESTION 2

Is it more important to fit in with your friends, or to be yourself? Discuss your answers.

WRITING PROMPT 1

What makes being part of a team fun? What makes it difficult? Do you prefer to do things on your own, or be a part of the team? Write about cooperation.

WRITING PROMPT 2

Imagine that Chester and Cora must compete to decide who will be team captain. Write a story about their competition. What happens? Who wins? You decide.

(AM-bush)—to hide and then attack someone

(KUHV-ur FIRE)—when you fire a paintball marker to distract your opponents and protect your teammates

(FOR-fit)—to be disqualified, or lose, because of a penalty or for doing something wrong

(IN-stingktz)—natural abilities

(KEEN)—sharp or alert

(MARK-ur)—a piece of equipment that fires paintballs

(MARKS-muhn)—someone who has really good aim

(puh-TROLL)—to walk or travel in an area to keep watch on people and scout their positions

(SKOUT)—someone sent to find out and bring back info

(TAK-tiks)—plans or methods to win a game or achieve a goal

CREATORS

SEAN TULIEN › *Author*

Sean Tulien is a children's book editor living and working in Minnesota. In his spare time, he likes to read, eat sushi, exercise outdoors, listen to loud music, and write books like this one. Sean has two scars from his own paintball experiences, but he still loves to play.

ABURTOV › *Illustrator*

Aburtov is a graphic designer and illustrator who has worked in the comic book industry for more than 11 years. In that time, Aburtov has colored popular characters like Wolverine, Iron Man, Punisher, and Blade. He recently created his own studio called Graphikslava. Aburtov lives with his beloved wife in Monterrey, Mexico, where he enjoys spending time with family and friends.

ANDRES ESPARZA › *Inker*

Andres Esparza has been a graphic designer, colorist, and illustrator for many different companies and agencies. Andres now works as a full-time artist for Graphikslava studio in Monterrey, Mexico. In his spare time, Andres loves to play basketball, hang out with family and friends, and listen to good music.

FARES MAESE › *Colorist*

Fares Maese is a graphic designer and illustrator. He has worked as a colorist for Marvel Comics, and as a concept artist for the card and role-playing games Pathfinder and Warhammer. Fares loves spending time playing video games with his Graphikslava comrades, and he's an awesome drum player.

WAIT!

DON'T CLOSE THE BOOK!
THERE'S MORE!

FIND MORE:

GAMES
PUZZLES
CHARACTERS

www.capstonekids.com